_____
Your name

Please draw a face
showing how you feel today.

Here is a picture taken last year of me with my mom and dad. See how happy we look.

What a lie! We were not happy at all.

*Please draw a picture of you
and the grown-ups you live with.*

My mom and dad used to go out drinking with their friends. Sometimes they would come home drunk.

Draw a picture of someone you have seen drunk.

I stayed in my room when Dad was drunk.
But sometimes he would get me anyway.
He'd say I needed to be taught a lesson.
Then he would slap me until my head rang.

What is a time you have ever been hurt by a grown-up? _____

The next day, Dad would say he was sorry.
He would promise that we would go fishing.
He'd say he wanted us to be good buddies.

I had heard this all before.
After hurting me, Dad would be nice for a time.
Then he would get drunk and hurt me again.
Dad wouldn't stop hurting me.

Why do you think grown-ups hurt kids?

Mom was afraid of Dad when he was
drunk. She also got upset because
he spent our house money on liquor.

Mom said I was just like my dad
—always causing trouble.
She acted like she hated Dad and me.

Mom seemed to think that
all her troubles were my fault.
She said she was sorry she had a kid.
Mom's words hurt just as badly as Dad's fists.

What is Mom saying?
What is Luis saying?

Mom told me not to tell anyone about Dad hitting me.
She said the police might put Dad in jail.
Then we wouldn't have any money to live on.
She said I deserved what I got.

What can happen to grown-ups who hurt children?

_____

When people asked about my bruises,
I said I had fallen off my bike.
I was afraid to tell the truth.
I didn't want to get Dad in any trouble.

What can happen to kids who tell on their parents?

Mom and Dad were always nice
around other people. Lots of kids thought
I was a very lucky guy.
I pretended my life was great.

What is something you pretend that is not true?

Sometimes I dreamed that things were different in my life. I had make-believe friends in a make-believe world.

What two wishes would you like to make about your life?

1) _____

2) _____

One day I asked Uncle Charley to tell Dad to stop hurting me. He said that my grandfather used to hit him and Dad.
That was the way kids were taught to grow up in our family.

What is another way kids can be taught other than hitting them?

I started acting like my dad.
When kids made me mad, I hit them.
One day I was suspended from school.

Tell about a time that you hurt someone.

When Dad learned I had been suspended, he punched me hard in my eye. The side of my face started to swell up big.

*W*hat is Dad saying?
What is Luis saying?

There was no way to hide the black eye.
My teacher also remembered
the bruises from before.
He sent me to see the school counselor.

How do you feel about talking to someone about your hurts? _____

The counselor asked me
about my bruises and black eye.
I told her I didn't want to talk about it.
She said there are both good and bad secrets.
Bad secrets hurt if we don't tell them.

*What would be a good secret that is OK to keep?*_____

What would be a bad secret that should be told? _____

I was scared, but I finally
told my bad secret to the counselor.
That was the bravest thing I have ever done.

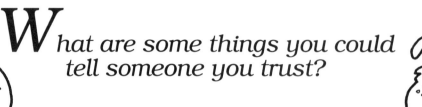 

*W*hat are some things you could
tell someone you trust?

Most of the time I feel _____

What bothers me the most is _____

_____

The reason it bothers me is _____

_____

Something I am afraid of is _____

_____

The reason I am afraid is _____

_____

My life would be better if _____

_____

The counselor said that I was not bad.
Neither were my mom or my dad.
It was not my fault that Dad got drunk
and Mom was unhappy.

My counselor said she would try to get
someone to help both me and my parents.

Who do you think could help your dad or mom?

What could anyone do or say to your parents that would help?

A woman from the child protection agency told Mom and Dad not to hurt me anymore. She said that it is against the law for grown-ups to injure children.

Mom and Dad agreed to get help in changing the way they treat me.

How would you like your parents to change?

Dad has started meeting with a support group where there are men and women who have stopped drinking. Now they help others.

What is the name of a support group you have heard of? _____

Mom and Dad started going to a counselor. They are learning to share their feelings. Then they won't need to hurt me when they get mad.

How would you feel if your parents went to a counselor? _____

I am going to a counselor, too.
She said kids have rights just like grown-ups.

My body is my own.
No one has the right
to injure me.

My mind is my own.
No one has the right
to make me hate myself.

How do you feel about yourself?

I am responsible for myself — my feelings and actions — NOBODY ELSE IS.

*Do you feel responsible for your parents?*_____

*Why?*_____

Telling my bad secret was the hardest thing I ever did. It was also the best thing.

Dad still gets mad, but he doesn't hit me.
Mom doesn't call me stupid anymore.
My life is not perfect, but it is much better.

Kids alone can't stop adults from hurting them. They have to get other grown-ups to protect them.

If you ask one person and they don't help, ask someone else. The sooner the better.

Name three safe grown-ups who might help you if an adult is hurting you.

1) _____

2) _____

3) _____